SWIFT MOVERS International

For my amazing parents—CM

PENGUIN WORKSHOP
An imprint of Penguin Random House LLC, New York

First published in the United States of America by Penguin Workshop, an imprint of Penguin Random House LLC, New York, 2024

Copyright © 2024 by Cherry Mo

Penguin supports copyright. Copyright fuels creativity, encourages diverse voices, promotes free speech, and creates a vibrant culture. Thank you for buying an authorized edition of this book and for complying with copyright laws by not reproducing, scanning, or distributing any part of it in any form without permission. You are supporting writers and allowing Penguin to continue to publish books for every reader.

PENGUIN is a registered trademark and PENGUIN WORKSHOP is a trademark of Penguin Books Ltd, and the W colophon is a registered trademark of Penguin Random House LLC.

Visit us online at penguinrandomhouse.com.

Library of Congress Cataloging-in-Publication Data is available.

Manufactured in China

ISBN 9780593661345   10 9 8 7 6 5 4 3 2 1 HH

Design by Mary Claire Cruz

This book is a work of fiction. Any references to historical events, real people, or real places are used fictitiously. Other names, characters, places, and events are products of the author's imagination, and any resemblance to actual events or places or persons, living or dead, is entirely coincidental.

The publisher does not have any control over and does not assume any responsibility for author or third-party websites or their content.

HOME in a LUNCHBOX

by Cherry Mo

Penguin Workshop

MONDAY

Hello!

Hel...lo!

What's your name?

你好 = Hello
謝謝 = Thank you
不知道 = I don't Know

?

Th...ank you...

RIIIINGGG

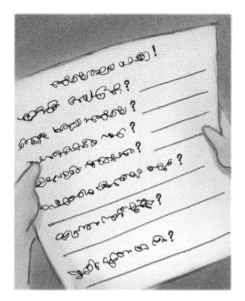

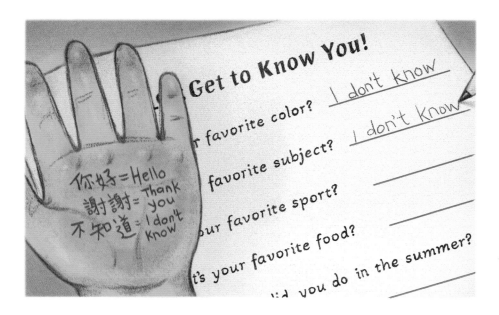

你好 = Hello
謝謝 = Thank you
不知道 = I don't know

Get to Know You!

favorite color? ___I don't know___

favorite subject? ___I don't know___

ur favorite sport? ___

t's your favorite food? ___

id you do in the summer? ___

囗厠 = Toilet
不客氣 = You're welcome
不知道 = I don't know

Toi...let?

he he he ha ha ha ha ha ha

he ha he he ha ha ha

ha ha he he he ha ha ha

WEDNESDAY

I pledge allegiance to the flag...

I...pleh...alee...

FRIDAY

THURSDAY

...

Wow...
um...
you...
uh...
um...

MONDAY

Hello!

That looks good!

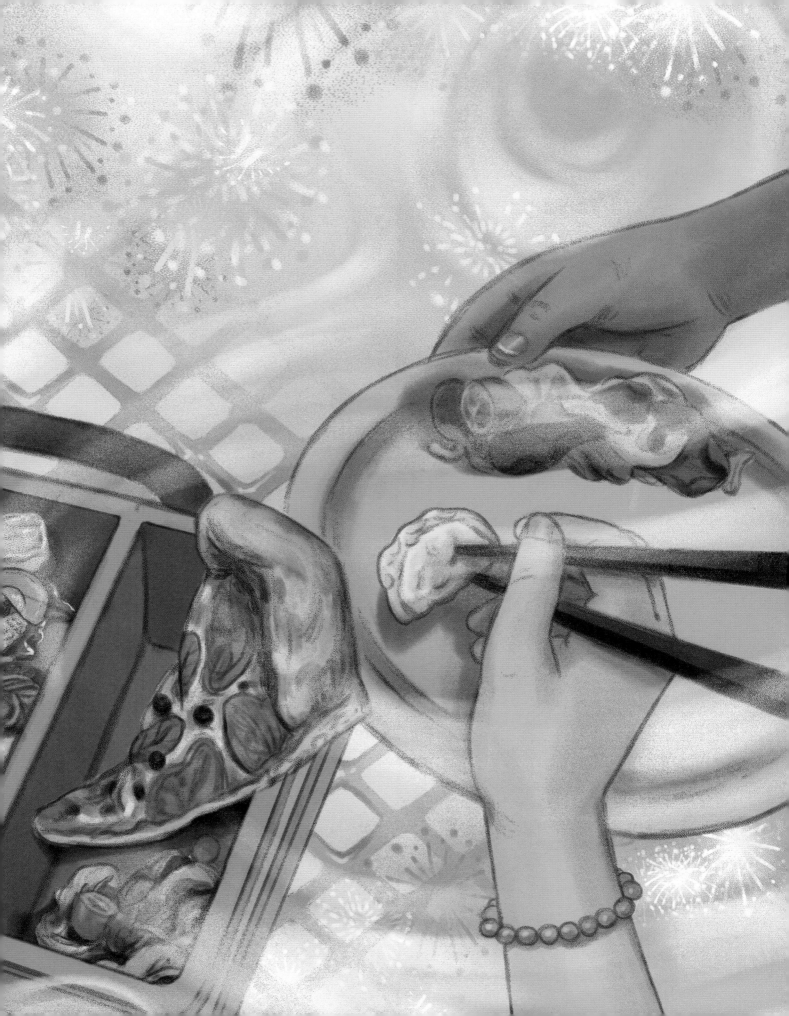

Yum!

Mmmm!

This belongs to: Jun

Thank you... Jun!

Rose.

Juan!

Daniel.

Thank...you, Rose, Juan, Dani...el!

What are the words on Jun's hand?

English	Written and Conversational Cantonese
Hello	你好 nei hou
Thank you	謝謝 Written: je je Conversational: doh je
I don't know	不知道 Written: bat ji dou Conversational: ng ji dou
You're welcome	不客氣 Written: bat haak hei Conversational: ng haak hei
Restroom (US) / Toilet (UK)	洗手間 / 廁所 sai sau gaan / chi soh

Since Jun is from Hong Kong, she learned the British way of saying "restroom," which is typically "toilet." Hong Kong was a British colony, so British English is commonly used there.

What is in Jun's lunchbox?

好食! Yummy!

Braised Tofu
紅燒豆腐 / Hung Siu Dau Fu

A popular Chinese dish with tofu and vegetables simmered in a savory sauce.

This belongs to: Jun

Bok Choy
白菜仔 / Baak Choi Jai

A type of green Chinese vegetable commonly used in stir-fry dishes.

Vegetable Bao
素菜包 / So Choi Baau

Steamed bun with a variety of vegetable fillings.

Mushroom Vegetable Dumpling
香菇蔬菜餃 / Heung Gu Soh Choi Gaau

Minced mushrooms and vegetables wrapped in a thin layer of dough.

White Rice
飯 / Baak Faan

A common food staple in the traditional Chinese diet.

Vegetable Chow Mein
雜菜炒麵 / Jaap Choi Chaau Min

Mixed vegetables such as broccoli, carrots, and bell peppers stir-fried with noodles.

Thousand Layer Pancake
抓餅 / Jaau Beng

Flaky, multilayer, savory pancake.

Sweet Red Bean Soup
紅豆沙 / Hung Dau Sa

A common Chinese dessert made with red mung beans, lotus seeds, and lily bulbs.